Parents and Caregivers,

Stone Arch Readers are designed to provide enjoyable reading experiences, as well as opportunities to develop vocabulary, literacy skills, and comprehension. Here are a few ways to support your beginning reader:

- Talk with your child about the ideas addressed in the story.

- Discuss each illustration, mentioning the characters, where they are, and what they are doing.

- Read with expression, pointing to each word. You may want to read the whole story through and then revisit parts of the story to ensure that the meanings of words or phrases are understood.

- Talk about why the character did what he or she did and what your child would do in that situation.

- Help your child connect with characters and events in the story.

Remember, reading with your child should be fun, not forced. Each moment spent reading with your child is a priceless investment in his or her literacy life.

Gail Saunders-Smith, Ph.D.

STONE ARCH READERS

are published by Stone Arch Books, a Capstone Imprint
1710 Roe Crest Drive
North Mankato, Minnesota 56003
www.capstonepub.com

Library of Congress Cataloging-in-Publication data
is available on the Library of Congress website.

ISBN 978-1-4342-4019-4 (library binding)
ISBN 978-1-4342-4237-2 (paperback)

Reading Consultants:
Gail Saunders-Smith, Ph.D.
Melinda Melton Crow, M.Ed.
Laurie K. Holland, Media Specialist

Designer: Hilary Wacholz

Printed in the China
032012   006677RRDF12

Field Trip for School Bus

written by
Melinda Melton Crow

illustrated by
Chad Thompson

STONE ARCH BOOKS
a capstone imprint

School Bus, Tractor, Fire Truck, and Train were friends.

Field Trip
Today!

School Bus was happy.

He was going on a field
trip to the zoo.

"Have fun!" said his friends.

11

School Bus picked up the
children.

13

They sang all the way to
the zoo.

School Bus sang, too.

"We are at the zoo!" said
School Bus.

The children were happy.

They saw lots of animals
at the zoo.

23

School Bus slept.

Soon it was time to go home.

"Thank you, School Bus!"

"You are welcome!"

STORY WORDS

friends	zoo	animals
field trip	children	slept

Word Count: 83